THE IMBOLC BRIDE

THE IMBOLC BRIDE

John Sewell

LITTLEWOOD ARC

Published by Littlewood Arc
The Nanholme Centre, Shaw Wood Road
Todmorden, Lancashire OL14 6DA

Poems © John Sewell 1992
Cover designed by Tony Ward
Printed at the Arc & Throstle Press
Nanholme Mill, Todmorden, Lancs.
Typeset by Anne Lister Typesetting
Brunswick House, South Street, Halifax

ISBN 0 946407 86 X

ACKNOWLEDGEMENTS
*Contemporary Yorkshire Poetry Anthology;
Giant Steps; Lancaster Literature Festival
Poetry Competition Anthologies '82, '87, '89, '90;
Mountain; National Poetry Competition
Anthology '89; New Welsh Review;
Observer; Other Poetry; Pennine Platform;
Poetry Nottingham; Poetry Review; Poetry
Supplement, Leicester Haymarket Theatre;
Prospice; Rialto; Staple; Yorkshire Post.*

Some of the poems have been broadcast on
Radio 3 'Poetry Now'; Radio Nottingham;
Radio Sheffield.

'The Fall' won First Prize in the York Open
Poetry Competition '86. 'Son's Dream' won
Third Prize in the South Yorkshire Poetry
Competition '84; 'Anna in Borrowdale, 1' won a
Runners Up prize in the National Poetry
Competition '89; 'Malmesbury' won Third Prize
in the Leek Poetry Competition '91.

Some of the poems have appeared in a limited
edition pamphlet: *Lunch on the Grass.*

The award of a Writers' Bursary from East
Midlands Arts is gratefully acknowledged.

The publishers acknowledge financial
assistance from Yorkshire and Humberside
Arts Board, North West Arts Board and
East Midlands Arts.

for Joannie

CONTENTS

THE CLIMBER AND THE WEATHERCOCK
St. Mary's Church, Bottesford

One Robt. Fease, in 1610,
ascended twice the crocketted spire,
curlicue to curlicue on the raking edge,
that took him up two hundred slender feet
into the turning swifts,
once to ease the weather vane to earth,
and once to set it hale into the winds.

For which work he received
three shillings and sixpence
and the wide gaze of the whole parish.

SEEDING THE CLOUDS

The day's so nice, I show up prompt by trees,
offer earth my excrement, my clouds of seed.
A pleasing act, my lower half in clay
my head in sky. The air, scenting secrecies,
announces in its wild high tail-up way –
Spring's back, his base magnificence laid bare!
The husks split clean, an early butterfly
swoons past, a new-lit dungfly plants his feet
into my dung, his share of my beneficance.
On the earth's clod studded with coltsfoot,
I learn his ecstasy, likewise sense with air
on my one wing, all wings' renewal.
First thorn and elder and quick sallow clothe me
then the chestnut, fanning like a peacock.

I

ONE YEAR ON
i.m. K.R.S.

He stepped out, saw strange colours on the world,
the lawn a stunning sheen of emerald,
the hills in close, faceted, brighter than he'd ever known.
The whole scene out of key, out of register, one thing
part shifted on the next, until the purple iris
fifty years had focused on, appeared
beyond themselves, the wind-honed fence posts – split.

Nights on end, gales swept in across the moor.
Walls always held, and woke to find sunlight.
But this came calm, flatstill, as if the sea had stopped,
a quiet for which the stonechat had no answer.

Fieldhouse

It's spring, the purple birches weathered
to a silver fume, our chimney smoke
a vapid blue against grey rock, the grate

piled high. I've split fresh logs, watching a blackbird
gather leaves into a secret place.
This morning, only rain, more rain, and wind

billowing the birch, its spawn of drips.
But through it – birdsong, in a plunge of spring,
I could high-kick toe to ceiling beam, one leg

then the other one, a second
touch, as something gives
inside my chest . . .

That spring came late. Almost May, then sudden snow –
trees arched full leaf, were snapped or lost
their poise, stayed permanently bent.

To die as flowering came – high June,
a flawless blue, the clarity remorseless,
field on field, a flourspill of maythorn.

Then the plummet into shadowed lanes,
time held apart, as if nothing
had been cancelled.

Waiting, almost for a word,
a prayer that is not a prayer,
tumbling towards me in the wind.

Reclaiming

He called it fate. Disorder multiplied.
His mind unwound in months to a baby's.

Seeds rotted. Rows grew weedstruck. While all around
were planting on, his plot regressed, became a web

of briar and thistle. I made a start
half-heartedly. His spade's grip smooth as glass.

Moor

I remember the dust of him, falling from my hand
down the wind in long slow arcs, the red strewn carnations.

This, as the sun touches down again, draining flat into that moor,
a score of swifts stitching at the sky, and one that dips and lifts

and dips again, so close its wingbeats dash and tremble into being.
One that day too along the edge, how it closed on us, then flew

beyond, snatched limb by limb into the air,
a vacancy instilled on every side. Now, in the contracted light

more remote and numinous than swift, absence of swift,
a breath of heartbeats, expectancy of its return.

Widow

No grave, we laid him into living air,
blowing east at evening to this garden
where the sweet peas stir and fluster – red, white
pennants from the trelliswork. They hardly rest
scarp-edged into a Pennine wind, that meant

chrysanthemums were broken at their stakes
and greenhouse panes shook flying down the path,
enough to make you weep at all the effort lost
in just one night, and facing it each morning
drawing back the blinds.

After the paid bills,
the pile of stock condolences,
to be outside and lifted in its blow
is like a blessing, feel every stitch of me
take shape. This August, how the sweet peas bloom.

Butterfly

Alive inside the house with me
and all the doors and windows shut,
– my mother speaking, letting words go free:
it gave me such a shock

to be alone, then hear it
flitting at the glass like that,
signalling its lovely wings.
I fetched a jar and set it free.

But the thought stayed on, and would not leave,
all day I couldn't help but think . . .
she didn't need to add *of him,*
the last words surfaced in her eyes.

I try to rationalise –
perhaps a door left half ajar,
a window in some upstairs room, but
simply the telling's brought her round.

Then next day, there it is
in my room now, the big sound
of its wings against a paper shade,
a fragile whispering between my hands.

Nothing stranger than weather needed here
to bring such chances into line,
yet something responds, deep, disquieting
as I open windows wider, let it free.

Homecoming
for Joannie

Three weeks love, you've been gone. The house
takes on a sober calm.
To the cat, it seems you'll not be back.
She looks to me for loving,
padding the bed at night, nudging at my hand.

I try to see his death like that – as someone
written off and not expected back. Though even
in dreams, with everything put right,
some tiny thing will hint prognostically at loss –
the sound of a shovel scraping on an empty yard.

But what if, like you, he was only held aside
by circumstance, planning a homecoming,
his figure at the door, and voice still solid
when the ringing stops. Cat thought. She stirs
from sphinx to fastening each hair in place.

Son and Daughter

At the sink –
screams of laughter,
thrown water scythes

mercurial
across the room.
We romp downstairs.

By the window
it rips home. To not
see him return

through the yard
mac
blackened in a downpour.

In a second
the spilt globs
overdarken everything.

New Year

Right, he said, it's nearly time.
We stepped outside, to the bite of the dark,
the lit house at our backs; stood
some little ways apart.

Soft ribbon of noise – glim of churchbells,
bagpipes phased on the wind, the flourish
as a rocket popped.

The intolerable instant of change.

Soaked bed, wasted limbs lifted out to the waiting
ambulance – become one now, with the framed snapshot,
the memory of his wish to dance.

The year's nape. The dock of the stars
gapes empty; no spent fall.
The world noses on. Two seconds part.
I cross the threshold.

Poppies

Out-palming hands – my father's poppies coming clear.
One summer, and they're settled here, celebrating
their event, their resurrection in a different ground.

We cope, if no one speaks, or sees us watching him
in their return. How long it takes, this easing out to
our thanksgiving, while theirs unhinges them.

Three days, and the soil's stunned red.

Next morning – seed heads, scallop-fisted, rising clear.
Defiance moving one step further, to a new perfection.
By the poppies now, a singing starts, so thin

I hear it only how we see in darkness,
looking to one side of things, standing slightly
aside the heart, under the dark uplift of trees.

Newborn

Nearly two weeks late and grown so big
    delivery was rending pain.
In the end they pulled him clear by force,
    like levering a tyre free.

He's sleeping while we come and go,
    to see whose chin he's got, whose hair,
and no one can resist just making sure
    he's real, by gently touching him.

Straight off, I saw *him* there, his sleep-shut face,
    the look he wore two days,
monitored, dead to everything
    beyond his heart-beat.

The eyes and nose are his, and his
    oblivion as deep, touching skin
and having nothing stir. And then to leave
    as we arrived, unseen, unheard,

through air-conditioned corridors
    walk out, uncomprehending
to the world; knowing this time
    he will live.

Re-run

I see tomorrow here, said Queequeg – the scene
from Moby Dick, where bones are cast on *Pequod's* deck.
Front stalls the first time, the *Majestic*

as a special treat, put us to sea. Me,
eight or so, too young for much beyond a tattooed face
or murderous waves. But you, near middle age,

would see it then: a throw of bone
and all tomorrows fallen out of place –
that day the doctor gave it to you straight.

Alone, not twelve months since you died, it's all still fresh,
watching, two decades on, the Great White rise
a second time, with Ahab lashed in torment to its flesh.

But it's the quiet, not the horror now, that stops me dead –
Queequeg, seated, seeing death breach up, as yours did,
on the mildest day, and nothing being said.

Song

I'm Gonna Sit Right Down And Write Myself A Letter

Fats Waller sings
Fats who died at 39 of too much booze
but well in front of life.
Fats who you loved and believed in
and sang along with in your boozy states
with your put-on baritone and your eyebrows
raised in wonder,
the pint glass in your hand swinging across your body
that is swaying not quite centred on the beat,
the whole assembly
hoisted lightly onto tiptoe.

Look, your prints are still there on the record sleeve
your voice still tracking his when his begins,
still missing when it soars or dips too far.

Listen, here's the part you liked
and this line coming, the way it turns around.

Listen, I am playing it again,
its sound is travelling outwards
like a clearing sky,
but faster than a sky can race.

And even you, the passing stranger,
even you who never knew us
may find yourself arrayed in light,
a song upon your lips,
though you stand unaccompanied
in the middle of swaying fields.

Son's Dream

A knock came to the door in the small hours.
        Don't answer it, I said,
I know that knock, I'll not go down to it.

        The phone rang then. Don't go
I said. I know who calls and I'll not answer.
        But the ringing came again

over and over, until I dressed and walked
        down night-lit streets towards that house.
There were sounds, the door swung back on light –

        a living room, where friends
and night-gowned neighbours danced, and there,
        by the piano, my father

shirt-sleeved, laughing. So exultantly undead.
        Beyond believing, what I
felt just then – full measure back into the world.

Only why had it taken so long?
        An uncle, barrels
out a song, my mother adds a trill.

        What's done is gone, and past.
Do I like his hair now, parted this way?
        Is all my father asks.

Raising His Name

Sans serif, sans finesse, all afternoon
on the dome of Bleaklow, carving stone,
the glowering, man-high capstone of the moor.
Smell of steel on skin. The chisel, ice-cold, jarred
and juddered in my hand, chipped rock flew loose,
the K lost all precision, the R and S
described ungainly curves. What mattered
was to etch in deep, add three raw letters
to the scores of others chiselled there.

Kinder, Ronksley, Shelf Moor – each grey ridge
bodies into view above the bristling drop
to firs, a lake's panned sheen of ore. And look!
two thousand feet below – as though he's still in sight,
in all that clear, wide-bellied sweep of dale –
his yellow oilskin bright about the yard . . .
Back down, I sink and glow, grow chilled and rise,
hearing from within, my mother's voice
announcing absently – *That's Ken come home.*

I turn towards an empty yard, then step inside.

II

THE IMBOLC BRIDE

Imbolc, on 1 February, was the Celtic festival associated with the rites
of prognostication and trial marriage. Young men and women would
gather, walk towards each other, kiss and be wed.

Presentiment   The hill at dawn. Boot strap of woodsmoke snake-lithes
into stillness. My thought each time

is reaching top, to see her there, her eyes on mine.
Might we make love?

This longing, if you would,
I would have it answered.

All that can, clasps hard around us,
and nothing changes. Hours pass.

I lay, shaped moss and fescue for a bed,
her fume musk impressed earthwards.

Meeting   Tall pines on the hill, my coat on the cold turf,
we plait our hair, become man and wife.

Parting at the roadside, snow fining down, no sound,
your wetness – its smell, a may-sprig on my hand.

Second moon of the new year, I dare not step outside
for wanting you, so beautiful the night.

Eclipse   The sky unbuckets ash, a black
stockade of trees, fields the snow's knocked flat.

Across bare grazing, head numbed with cold,
emptied, dulled, my single line of steps unrolls.

Too much beyond myself – was one friend's theory;
Just the time of year – was my reply;

31

to you I write-there seems at times
no brilliance left but yours.

Realisation How could you not be to love
as flesh is to its colouring – inseparable.

Kissed, it rises in you, winestaining
the skin of your neck, your chin

already pinked with beard chafe.
You dream awake.

Another love steals over you
in honeyed middle night.

Loss It hooks in far that kiss.
For what seems months, to wake up drained

of every other thought. And this,
that none who come can match that quake

and flush of pink. You –
lifting back the sheets

to see him leave,
to moonpale out on blue.

View of a Lake, Light tones predominate – blue spinnakers of sky;
Morning while underneath – dark shades,

the water's underskim sinks uncontained;
the two locked tight.

Reflection – one upon the other,
as close as could be hoped for, near perfect.

32

And a white house, off centre,
on the hillside, reaching out

continually for the eye, its small flourescence
sheeted into place on red bracken.

SAMHAIN

1
The apple, taken in two hands –
halved.
Summer; winter.
Tonight, for a few brief hours
they co-exist.

Outside, the wood in beech glow.
Thrust of cold
through the wind-bared ash.
Here, fire warmth
a curtained room.

The year ends; the year begins.
Fresh flame on a new candle.
A shiver, flesh to flesh.
It could be summer,
our two halves – bared, meeting.

2
Our bodies – yours, so perfect on the bed
I trembled taking hold;

which unmanned mine, only the mind held,
thrilled in its nakedness.

FATALITIES

Why, they wonder, is it For Sale again
so soon. They soon regret they ever asked.

While he talks he kicks the ground and looks aside,
gone through it now so many times, it seems
like someone else's life not his. The mess
of grief swept somewhere out of sight.

Slowly, he conducts you through events – wet roads,
control lost on a bend, the car thrown upturned
like a drawer, things smashed, strewn everywhere.

Her only crash, their marriage five nights off,
too late to cancel some things out, or calculate
the final cost. That's why he's selling up,

wants rid of dreams, the cold half-finished rooms
he walks you through. Then leaves,
drives nightwards down a labyrinth of lanes,
tears past three cars despite oncoming glare.

Do chances matter now, when every move she made
still led her there – that road, this corner
neither would have faced alone, and without
the other, might yet have made it round.

*

*Two cars back, they see the blood and dice
of shattered glass. Drive home,
returning safe this time. He garages
the car, comes in to find her
at the door, wanting his arms, in a room
luck fills for them with light.*

EIGHT PICTURES

for Joannie, Rowan and Freya

1 Halloween Lanterns

I saw ourselves in them, a pumpkin – you,
the turnip – me. All week I mused on us
displayed there as a pair. Love's themes were obvious –
a couple sculpted by a single hand, to suit
the other, burning with the same bright flame.
But differences too, where you are smooth
and rounded smiles; I scowl, gap-toothed, clodded from birth.
You dream of children, warmth, a home,
I see what's just gone wrong. Like only now
when needling wind blew through my snarl
and snuffed the magic out; while your laughter spills on
clean across the yard, lights up in one
the whole houseside.
                    Love, answer me this much,
Did you see this too and saying nothing, smile?

2 Nativity

The physics of love –
a needle of pethidine
sunk into her thigh,
the aquasonic heartbeats
of the child.

Pain. The livid birth-tear
set to split.
Mucus, sweat.
A midden smell.
The bed a soiled yard floor.

Pain fogs the room of faces.
She is alone under the night,
dry mouthed,
inheriting the miracle.
Her body, her suffering – his instrument.

The stars beyond
as we have never seen them.
Sharp and clear – her cry, his cry,
and all else lost
the instant he appears, closed eyes,

blood-daubed in her arms,
her whole face fastened down on his.

3 Rowan

Blood splats on floor tiles
             pink drifts of the spilt
blossom, my peony-headed one
             falls warm across the breast
his dazzlement and mine
             cuticle of new leaf
tree-swirl of swallows
             a fresh-sprung fleck of lark
each word, hand, leaf
             new dipped, ripples on glass
of window moon
             morning coltsfoot
cloudless on the bank
             vapour of soundless jet
the rowan's branches
             flex and spread
the garland bluster
             of that first red cry.

4 Wildfire in August

His shrieks crowd upward through the floor,
the ground's disturbed in every room.
By noon, it takes one word from you
to turn me blazing through the door.

On hillsides, fireweed takes light,
a spreading rouge of pink and rose,
first touch of all that follows –
leaf and flowerhead alight

dry-tindered to a twist of brown.
Through field-heat and the cool-swathed wood
pace slackens; stops, where cotton seed
spores from the hill, to view the town –

roof haze, spire, the patch of ground
half earth, half lawn, that must be ours,
and you, the child hooked in your arms
grown still, about to turn around.

5 The Fall

Curious of what I stoop for in the dark,
one second he's by me on the cellar step, the next
we're staunching panic from his eyes, the blood that bells from
                                                    his mouth.

He will not eat or drink, just clings and clings as a fever
twists him. The lamp outside starts pink, grows sulphureous.
He turns once like a dead weight in his cot, and sleeps.

His eyes, shadows in a shadowed face, seem to stare through
                                                 closed lids
to where we stand, taking in the bitter ruttle
of his throat, the spasms tangling at each limb.

He will not die, and yet there's death enough
in seeing him like this. What strickens us, is just how much
one second might erase, or need long weeks and months to
                                                 mend,

how we are fortunate, as well as mortified.
I walk out for air, through the dark-hedged lanes,
frayed light of an October moon

half smeared away by mist, low to the south,
scarcely higher than the hill it's lifted from.
Tomorrow is his eighteenth month alive.

She

Holds me
strokes me, loud and
fast, her heart on mine, fire
brats, our backs wet silver,
she whispers – press
press harder.

Nine months. Her waters drench the bed. Groans,
the ribboned birth trickle.
My urging – push
push harder.
And the head crowned,
the body, swathed in womb lard, flipped out
onto hers – a girl, a woman. I hold her and I hold her.

7 Morning Feed

Each day, a fresh pint
added gently, (not shaken).

Milk breath, if you get down close
the oatmeal of her scalp.

Already she is covering
her own tracks,

overprinting history
before our eyes.

8 Freya

Her face and mine in the mirror,
her cheek pressed to mine. She smiles.
She's three, I'm forty.

Her face, half the size, half as brown.
I'm thinking, how could I possibly
want more than this.

She hugs me at the neck, tight, says:
This is a picture.

III

HAWSE END

The slipway is rain-wet concrete
the same tone as the lake,
grey with rain, lapping the shore,
its shingle flushed red with the spent needles
of an overhanging pine.

A couple are haunched
beneath an oak
sheltering.

A launch draws by.
The man moves to the shore-line, waves.
Is this our boat? – he turns to me.
I cannot help.

The launch slows, veers into the bay.
Now on the slipway, at the jetty's end
he is grabbing for the rail, pulling the boat
against the last wooden upright.
They step aboard, enter the lit cabin,
are off, around the headland, out of sight.

Beside the one tall pine –
three other trees on the shingled point –
two oaks, one birch,
arched and lithe as the pine is straight.
They gesture, bend towards the lake,
downsweep movements balanced and contained.

The shore-line answers, with a long, slow arc.

ANNA IN BORROWDALE

1 Brown Slabs Arête, Shepherd's Crag
for Gill and Terry

Doors opened on an elm-flock of finches,
a wren churring in the crop of the ditch.
Hear the landscape, you said, from today the valley
has a new dimension. The slab's long back
lifted from the trees, a tinsmith's chink of karabiners,
rocks speaking: *taking in – ready – climbing now.*

It seems impossible, but yesterday
you hitched a rope, a yellow snake-rope,
round my waist, and drew me after you, on holds
my toes and fingertips could barely penetrate.
Each lift strained and powered me – a so-called
easy traverse, left across the wall. Half way

we belayed, spot danced on a ledge of rock,
air lake fields beneath us, wrinkling winds.
Keep to the crest mind, you said, then stepped out
round the arête, and disappeared. For minutes
the rope sighed after you. You became a voice,
the rock talking: *taking in – climb when ready.*

Climbing now, my foot and hand groping unseen holds.
I hugged that roll of rock, feeling the rope
like a fifth limb, fix me. The first moves, were the first moves
ever. I babystepped each one. From there, it all
came sweet, successional, the moves almost familiar.
At the top, my hand rushed into yours . . .

When you left, I cried. The house so empty.
Baby-cries of new lambs in the fields (the mother in me
starting up each time). How like love it felt, or some
devotion, scrambling fans of scree to reach the crest
the long way round. How dizzying this time
when jackdaws flip-dived out two floors below me.

Coming down, jays screeching for the trees, I saw
what we'd heard gunning from across the lake –
two spotted woodpeckers, working the birch,
fastened to the bark like brooches, their black and white
stained red as wounds, a seepage just above
the nape, a haemorrhage underneath the belly.

I harp on loss. From the spare room window,
hear the bright steel sing on Little Chamonix.

2 Lodore Falls
for Jude

Another element, another separateness.
Sluice of weather, of four days rain thrashed white
between rocks, a constant tinnitus of sound
reaching out over the hill to meet me
paused above the dale, above flood's aftermath –
a lost gleam, the lake's new acres shrunk back
into fields, our mudprints still there by the path.

I half expected you to turn me down.
Imagine how I felt when bold with wine
you said outright the very words I had in mind.
Eye to eye for minutes on end, hands cradling
the other's face. I was netted, held aloft
in blinks of tree light, a parabola
of earth-thing aired into weightlessness.

That's why I found myself (how many times)
beside these falls, letting sound beat through me,
drum away all thought, staring down into the flow,
deep bubbled, sliding like thick cords of oil.
Then seeing it – one stone among the many,
and clambering, to kneel, mid-stream, on a rock,
plunge a bare arm deep into the pool.

A stone of perfect roundness, blue
and discus-smooth, large enough to span one hand
from wrist to fingertips, and heavy
aching through sinews as I brought it back
and laid it by the fire – to bring you home.
Outside was starred and still, high in the dark,
the water's long, unbroken leap.

CLEAR MORNING, BORROWDALE

That night your dream
was one long search
that wouldn't reach me.

9 a.m. A reed stem
ice-armoured, faints
in stillness. The moon

wall-eyed, rimed on blue
above Bull Crag.
Cobalt rattle of magpies.

The sleep-print of sheep –
moss green on frosted fields.
Even the lake, trap-still,

edge-fixed with ice,
its own Skiddaw, a perfect
double, white for white –

I could have cried
finding myself here
at last.

We woke. Pressed together.

TIME-LAPSE, BRANDLEHOW

Our first house,
its cornerstone inscribed by you
    that long hot afternoon,
our four initials
    wedded into three:
    R F
      H   1763

They could be us two, starting over,
this couple
    walking through the rain
towards us, up the mudded track.

Instantly, she sees us clearly,
    with such bright affinity,
and now, he too –
    his finger tracing yours
    across the incised stone.

They're not at ease.
You can see she's still unsure
    of their connection.
Remember the hollow, where the track
    meets the beck.
It's still a mire.
You carried me across that time.

Now she's declining the same offer,
    risks the mud,
balancing on stones and stooks of earth.

She falters,
    and his hand grips hers
    for a moment only,
but you can feel that touch
    fuse them closer.

She's safely over,
saying almost the same thing
    as I said then –
I was afraid of you,
    now can't imagine why.

AUGUST VANISHING

An almost imperceptible
elision in the leaves, the jading
of some long, unstated promise.

The first grey-headed morning, grasses
fogged and hennaed,
the ash tree swagged with seed.

In the yard, nothing
        but the stink of sheep.
All summer the hot zinc shadow of the barn
arboured them from heat. Empty now.

A light breeze shakes the meadow. Seep
of sweat, a storm of spinning flies. Step
by step – field to willowherb to wood.

A swirl of crows rises
        from nowhere
on a hawk.
North, they harry it

it seems for miles, over the sheep-land,
jinking, twisting,
lean wing under heavy wing
        black wing over bronze.

DOG FOX DEAD ON A YARD WALL

slung from a hook, cord
tight round hind legs, flanks
divotted, mud-welts
on the wheat-cream belly, root flash
of brush, tipped flat
along the spine, his whole weight
in traction on that hook, snout,
front pads edging
to outstretch his dive, defy
the sheer
                    incomprehensible
                                        perfect
countermovement of the earth
away from him,
while he hangs leaping

above dandelions and asphalt
inching slowly into cover.

WHITE POPLARS

All week, a yellow wind strikes north
through the poplars, thins them
leaf by leaf, to armature
and wire, artless things
abandoned on the hill.

In June, I watched a green wind plunge
the river, tilt the trees, toss them
like a flipped umbrella outside in.
Each leaf became its whitened underleaf,
a lime-blanched ghost.

The whole tree fluxed, new blossom thickened,
shone and faded, in one brief
snatch-second gust of spring . . .
Late autumn now. Downwind a leaf-mat
rags the field, flattened leaves

press downwards on their own shadows,
each canker-splattered with its drop of black,
a mouth, a sink-hole
through which leaf, field, year is draining,
hurrying as it empties.

LATE EVENING, BORROWDALE

A dust of midges.
Half light thins the visible.
I stand a long time turning everything around.

There should be one place
where, when the worst happens,
you will always be received.

It's dark when I get back, lift the latch
and let light spill into your room.
Too late.

I say your name, but you don't stir.
Stab the fire into stars, into dross
until it's gone.

Outside the air's astringent –
bog myrtle crushed in the hand.

DERWENTWATER

The lake is round. It speaks
arrival.

There's a ruffling of water,
a high, thin sifting of trees.

That person, who sits facing the lake
on a seat that speaks of someone's

vanished life, grows older each time.
Each time, this same unchange –

the line of gold and broken reed
at the water's rim, a ruffling of air.

And all his vanished lives still round him,
speaking their own arrival,

as if it were today they came,
to sit, facing the lake.

The lake that is round. And speaks
only of arrival.

ULLSCARF

No stroll this, across the fell
sunlight at your heels;
but sun, receding into rain,
foregrounds darkening, the wind's jab
and the land stubbed featureless.

Only there, sleeked in the valley's haunch,
the light-gleam of a lake –
grace notes of a phrase
whose meaning, familiarity
has almost worn away.

SKIDDAW

Someone had heard it from someone else, that he'd been dead an hour,
a heart attack, some fifty feet below the summit.

There had been that sharp ascent, 1 in 2 or more, from Millbeck
to Broad End; a day that at long last, would keep its promise.

Breathless, iced with sweat, on the last push up, I passed this group,
some stretched out, some standing to one side; I saw one woman

gently kiss a man who had his arms held loose about her.
Once past, I rounded on the summit, gaining pace and strength.

The crest, the cairn, and all the north beyond, greened up in front,
and there, out of the blue, heading straight for me, its rhythmic beating

growing ever louder, a yellow rescue helicopter, that slowed
and swung above me, then hovered with a roar below the ridge.

Back I went, to see the port doors open, a body
being winched inside, and foil, whole sheets of it, swept skywards

from the scree by the thrash of rotors, each flung strip glinting
as air made light of it, a sliding, tumbling shim of brightness.

IV

BOGART DIES

That old rumour! Don't those guys check the facts.
I had a slight malignancy in the esophagus;
they wrote that half my lungs had been removed,
with half an hour to live, and every cemetery
from here to Tulsa rolling out the mats for me,
including some, I know for sure take only dogs.
I need to gain a little weight that's all.

They helped him dress. Aurilio, downstairs, tugged the ropes,
the dumbwaiter, with its top removed, started down,
Bogie seated inside on a stool.
The shaft was dark. The drop took twenty seconds.
Endless. Like that night he walked back into town
along the highway, away from everything,
Mayo back there, drunk on board *The Sluggy.*

It was 4 a.m. when headlights slowed towards him,
in his rope-soled shoes, hands shielding his eyes,
near desperate, shouting: *Betty, is that you ..?*
Outside, the pool shuffled its diamonds,
the polished marble of the patio glared up blindingly.
Already it hurt like hell. He held a glass,
a cigarette. It was a little after five.

BERMUDAS

The 17th May we saw change of weather and had much rubbish
swimme by our shipside whereby we knew we were not far from land.
Log of The Deliverance, 1610.

1

Five hours at thirty thousand feet,
over cloud floe and a white flecked sea,
to reach that fish-hook skliff of land,
its circled reefs that crack the ocean
into distillates of blue and green,
the blue arc of a welder's flame –
sea light poured into the breeze through oleander,
palm and cedar, where the kiskadee
calls out its name over lawns and rooftops
of the lime washed villas, every one
with patio and pool, a rottweiler
collared to a paw-paw tree. Hear that laughter?
The Butterworths next door are giving brunch
this Easter Sunday, to friends in swimwear, bronzed
exiles from a harsher clime. Their kids launch kites,
acid mauves and yellows ripple into light,
but no one's watching – all grow tired
of such delights. Soon the kids will race inside,
stack the CD player with sixties hits,
while Fraser, by a hedge of red hibiscus,
flips the burgers, bastes on a little more
Buffalo Bobs Bar B Que Bracer,
says – *Brenda knocked it back last night,*
God, did she look green! The buns – brown, white,
relish-tongued, lie open mouthed on every plate.
Best move I ever made – to sell my yacht,
twelve thou' clear we made. Is that enough
on yours. Say honey, where's that Lestoil stuff,
the kids have beach tar on their feet.
Where are they? In the house! Oh shit.
Meanwhile, somewhere above, the inflight
movie's through. A stewardess
hands long haul mums, now the kids are fed

and finally asleep, free champers
that the Club Class left. The queue lengthens
for the toilets aft, as warning lights
alert three hundred souls to fasten seat belts
they'll be landing soon, and thanks to all
for a pleasant flight. Wing tips tremble
over turbulence, the Tri-Star dips
and shudders, as they make their slow descent.

2
The sun was moving to its exultation.
The Welcome Mat said HI! COME IN.
You must be a Taurus, the hostess said,

just the man we need! – However did you guess? I said.
But she was busy splitting the room into seven,
ready for the big adventure. We took the clues:

Find ONE – under sentence of water torture.
TWO – labyrinthed in Tom Moore's hat.
A tourist will sign you THREE, near Spanish Point.

The idea seemed to be – fragments of a treasure map
lay stashed around the island, in drainpipes, trees.
The task – locate each piece, spot X, and win!

– Or fail! I tipped the fall from bull to bear. Beth
the daughter of the house, offered a smile,
a clew of thread: *Mom could tell by the legs of course,*

*that bleached effect; the fact we don't wear shorts
till start of May!* The door-yard was a maze
of topiary, small chocolate eggs glinted

from each branch. The kids were going wild, melted
treasure smeared down faces, T-shirts, hands.
We took our only chance – the grand evasion –

grabbed a youngster each -- oh the exculpation.

3

As you'd pictured it – an oval pool
the blue light dancing,

and the clean cut of a dive
bubble-pelted,
3, 4, 5, before he surfaces
hair slicked black.

One dive's enough,
he siloes out, ballistic grace,
goes   slap   slap   slapping past,
to plant himself beside the bar.

At night, the pool's a lit vat,
cool irradiated blue,
one lamp below the surface
swims a length   and back.

The lawn's deserted, dark.
There's an echo of a slap
against the side. Mars burns red
in the pool's cold depth.

Dive – I dare me –
dive.

4
Here Sam Fowel, sailor, drowned
in 1840. Grassy Bay –
such a mild green place.

I snorkel there
on a curved ocean, star-shadow
drifting over sea fans, jades and purples,

slip under, down,
feel a mild push (like the sough
of curtains on the night) as a wave

breaks over, and a vein of cold
slides in. It was then
I boiled to the surface, gulping

the garish sky, scared, suddenly
by an easefulness
of motion, the sight of coral

in my death-white hand.

5

Globe lights mazed the water by the jetties,
the fancy yachts were clinking at their berths,
we were two couples, two philosophies –
Thatcher and the creaking apparatus
of the Welfare State, sat down together
at the Buena Vista (Guests and Members) Club.
This evening our Sommelier suggests
Margaux Barton, Mouton Cadet. Dave says
Whatever, urges Mrs T. go the whole way –
INSIST we ALL invest in our own good health.
I counter with the usual plea – compassion
and the common good, pushed that for starters –
Crab Newburg in Pastry Shell, Sevruga
Caviar, and something else I can't recall.
From that point on things really hotted up.
You'll be saying next, I said, *the government*
should boil down all the long term unemployed,
promote their productivity as glue
or poultry feed – after all, she's let them stew
this long since she snatched office!
                          – Oh come off it,
don't talk WET! A waiter, setting match
to the Pheasant Flambé gave us all a moment's
pause, then it was onward, ever on –
Darwin versus Faith; Doing Well for One's Self
v. Institutional Conspiracies;
on, with voices rising, to and beyond
Blueberry Blintzes, Savarin Royale.
Did that sate us? Did it hell! *This* was personal.
He – was greedy, moved here only to save tax.
I – was pitiable, would never move beyond
my cosy street. God, I was weak.
          Silence after that. The after-coffee mint
refused. Likewise, the offer that he pay,
it being pricey and his treat. No way
I'd let *that* pass. I paid our share, down to the last

69

extra portion of Baked Alaska.
We saw ourselves out after that. Thereafter
it was back to ground beef on a bun –
Sam's Mobile Lunch Counter, parked by the fence
near the Container Berth, end of Front Street.

6
And the god in this machine?
The god of Marvell's wonders?

He's in the tree frogs,
the pulse in the thorn bush
at the window;

in the longtails,
sweeping the last sea-drafts
to and fro;

in the shell burst
of palms against a darkening sky;
in violet navigation lights

out there alone above the reef,
the island a blister of small lights
strung across the waves.

But most of all
he's in the white tower
on the high hill of the island,

its thousand ribs and plates
shipped here and assembled
piece by iron piece,

the polished prisms of an eye
coast round on mercury
each fifty seconds.

All night he winks
into the room
to see that all is well.

And everything's just fine;
tomorrow we fly home.

*Frying tonight! Francis Knight, 25, of Wallasey, is to open
the first-ever fish and chip shop on sun-kissed Bermuda.*
Daily Mirror, 1989.

MALMESBURY

for Pauline Stainer

1
Who hasn't dreamt it?
To self-launch out
into swirling air.

1010 AD, the world's first
authenticated aeronaut,
Elmer the Monk,

makes a glider of himself
from the West Tower,
takes a long time

stealing up
to the wind's agitation,
the inrush of rashness.

He swoops a furlong,
breaks both legs, for ever,
but survives.

The back just needs a tail,
he said later, *Next time . . .*
But the Abbot knew best.

Elmer pondered the stars
into old age, had notions
no mortal soul could share –

the first lame cleric to the moon.

2

I thought of you Pauline, and that steely moment,
how your lines would stack it higher –
the bride on the steeple, the trembler on the aqueduct.

I puffed us up to heaven once – twin moons
to Jupiter: the god's cupbearer and the divinely
gifted nymph – consigned together in timeless orbit.

From the first, our's had something of the vertiginous
about it, an ordered fall neither could resist.
This morning, you watched me lean from the window

on whorls of frost, then shiver
and come back to you. Tonight, you call me out
from the kitchen – *Look! See them. Side by side!*

I see, through a trembling lens, our difference
narrowed to a fine slightness. There,
faint by the planet's disc –

Ganymede and Callisto both,
or one of them, alone in endless space.

3

We're circles you say,
that graze the other
continually.

That time on the coast
you tried paragliding
and the clip gave,

so you landed way off
course, almost hitting
the hotel roof.

You wrote afterwards,
it was sheer elation,
a Keatsian sensation

of air against bare skin.
When I take your hand
it's small in mine.

The grip is tight.
We stand a moment –
poised

JOHN SEWELL was born in South Yorkshire in 1950. Whilst studying architecture at Strathclyde he won the university poetry competition and co-produced a pamphlet called *Babel*. An East Midlands Arts Bursary in 1985 was followed by offers of publication. Alas, no collections were forthcoming but poems appeared widely in the national press and periodicals. In 1987 he was a finalist in the Arvon Poetry Competition, an editor for *Staple* magazine and a member of Peak Poets. In 1990 he appeared in *New British Poets 2* (Poetry Review) and won the Ilkley Festival Competition in 1991.

He now works as a conservation architect in the Peak District National Park, living in Bakewell.